The NEW BEAR at SCHOOL

For Dr. Elizabeth Marsden — always a smile. — C.W.

For the amazing Early Years Team at Piddle Valley. Thanks for everything! — T.W.

Text copyright © 2007 by Carrie Weston
Illustrations copyright © 2007 by Tim Warnes

All rights reserved. Published by Scholastic Press, an imprint of Scholastic Inc. *Publishers since 1920.*
by arrangement with Oxford University Press, Oxford.
SCHOLASTIC, SCHOLASTIC PRESS, and associated logos are trademarks
and/or registered trademarks of Scholastic Inc.

No part of this publication may be reproduced, stored in a retrieval system,
or transmitted in any form or by any means, electronic, mechanical, photocopying,
recording, or otherwise, without written permission of the publisher.
For information regarding permission, write to Oxford University Press,
Great Clarendon Street, Oxford OX2 6DP.

Library of Congress Cataloging-in-Publication Data
is available upon request.

ISBN-13: 978-0-545-05783-7
ISBN-10: 0-545-05783-3

10 9 8 7 6 5 4 3 2 1   08 09 10 11 12
Printed in China
The text type was set in Extreme

First American edition, July 2008

*With thanks to Michael Bond and HarperCollins for their kind permission
in allowing Paddington Bear to make three and a bit appearances in this book.*

Carrie Weston • Tim Warnes

The NEW BEAR at SCHOOL

Scholastic Press • New York

0 1 2 3 4 5 6 9 10
zero one two three four five six seven eight nine ten

The day that Miss Cluck said there was going to be a new animal in the class, everyone was very excited.

Monday

Wednesday

Thursday

day

1p

2p

milk 5p

Tuesday — BORIS!

music box ♫

REGISTER

When Miss Cluck said that
the new animal was a **bear**,
the other animals squealed
with delight.

Fergus — Monday!!
Wednesday!!
Friday!!

Today is

Tuesday

The weather is

Leticia the rabbit wondered if it might be a fluffy pink bear, like the one on her lunch box.

Maxwell the mole wanted a floppy brown bear with velvet paws.

The mice hoped for a bear in Wellingtons and a blue coat.

Fergus the fox cub thought any teddy bear would be just fine.

So, when the classroom
door opened

and Miss Cluck
introduced Boris,

everyone . . .

screamed!
For Boris wasn't a teddy bear.

He was an enormous, hairy, scary grizzly bear!

Miss Cluck told Boris she'd give him his uniform tomorrow, and found him a seat next to Maxwell.

But as he sat down, there was a loud **crack.**

It made Maxwell hide his face in his paws.

"Oh, Boris!" said Miss Cluck. "Why don't you sit on the floor instead?"

Miss Cluck gave Boris
a new book and a pencil.
He was very
proud indeed.

With a big, friendly grin, Boris turned to show the mice.

But Boris
forgot how
fierce
his teeth
were.

He forgot how
big
his paws
were.

And he forgot how **sharp** his claws were.

Somehow, the mice got scattered across the classroom.
Somehow, the pages of his new book got ripped.

Somehow, there was panic everywhere.

"Boris is too big!" cried one little mouse.

"Boris is too hairy!" yelled another.

"Boris is too scary!" they all squeaked together.

"Oh, Boris!" said Miss Cluck. "Please try to be more careful."

At lunchtime everyone sat together.

There was not enough room on the bench
for Boris, but nobody moved over.

So he sat all by himself
and dipped his big paw
into the large jar of
honey his mommy
had packed
for him.

When lunchtime was over
Miss Cluck said everyone
could go off and play.

The mice began a game of hide-and-seek.

"1 . . . 2 . . . 3 . . ."

Everyone ran to find a place to hide. But Boris was too **big.**

So Boris shut his eyes and counted instead.

"One . . . two . . . three . . .
coming to get you,"
Boris boomed.

"Eeek!"   "Stop!
Stop!"   "No!
No!"

?

Maxwell ran
crying to
Miss Cluck.

"Let's go inside and play
some quiet games,"
said Miss Cluck,
"and Boris, **please** try
to be less scary, dear."

red

orange

blue

purple

yellow

green

Fergus

Leticia

Maxwell

Monty Mouse

Marcus Mouse

Murray Mouse

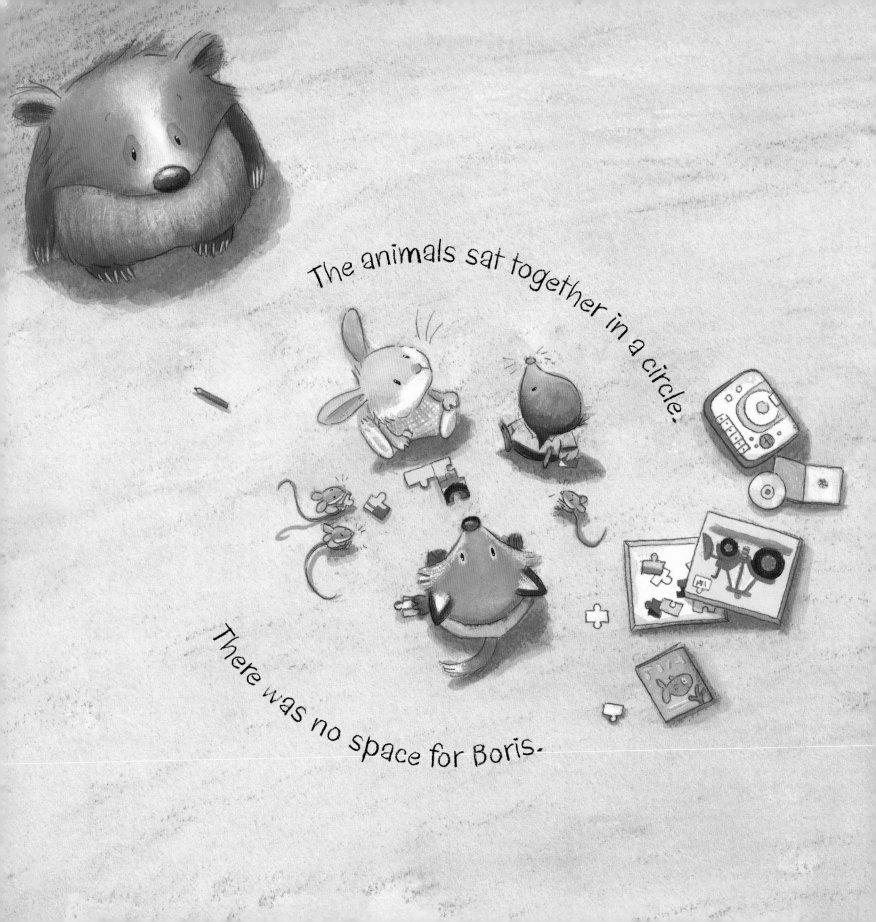

The animals sat together in a circle.

There was no space for Boris.

Boris had nobody to play with and nobody to talk to.
Tears filled his big, brown eyes, rolled down
his long nose, and splashed to the floor.

"I'm a
scary bear,"
he sniffed.

"I'm a
hairy bear,"
he sobbed.

"I'm just a great
big
grizzly bear."

It seemed like a very long afternoon.

At last it was time to go home.

Miss Cluck stood and waved as the animals set off through the woods.

Leticia hopped along the bank.

Fergus chased the little mice around a tree.

Maxwell scampered through the leaves.

Boris plodded along far behind.

Suddenly, from a hollow tree leapt....

the
rat
pack!

"Well, well, if it isn't the **crybabies,**" said the meanest rat.

poke!

"Help!"

Leticia, Maxwell, Fergus, and the mice trembled while the rat pack circled around them.

The rats didn't see Boris plodding along the path.

All Boris could see was lots of excitement ahead.

He wanted to join the fun.

Boris stood up tall to greet the new friends with his **biggest,** widest bear grin and . . .

The rotten rats ran away as fast as
their skinny legs could carry them.

"But I only wanted to
say hello. . . . ." called Boris.

When Boris turned around,
the other animals cheered.

"Boris is a hairy bear," they sang.

"Boris is a scary bear," they chanted.

"We're so glad that
Boris is our grizzly bear!"

Suddenly, Boris felt very shy.
"If you're going to be a bear,"
he said very gently,
"then it's probably best to be a
hairy, scary grizzly bear."

The next day at school, the animals couldn't wait to tell Miss Cluck how Boris had saved them from the nasty rat pack.

"Oh, Boris!" said Miss Cluck. "What a good bear you are."

At story time everyone rushed to gather around Miss Cluck. There wasn't much room once Boris had sat down.

But the rest of the class didn't mind one little bit. . .

. . . they all had a soft,
warm place to sit, after all!